I0830236

THE CROW
AND
THE PITCHER

A Retelling of Aesop's Fable

THE CROW
AND
THE PITCHER

A Retelling of Aesop's Fable

Written and Illustrated

by

Zeph Ernest

Ernest, Zeph
The Crow and the Pitcher: A Retelling of Aesop's Fable
ISBN: 978-0-578-53757-3

Produced in the United States of America

Dedicated to

the indomitable spirit.

Contents

Preface   vii

Chapter 1   1

Chapter 2   4

Chapter 3   13

Glossary   20

Author Biography   24

Preface

The Crow and the Pitcher *is one of approximately 150 fables credited to Aesop (620–564 BCE). Some writers believe Aesop is from Ethiopia, and others think he is of Greek origin. However, given the number of African animals in the fables, the evidence is overwhelming that he was an African storyteller, or the stories originated in Africa. Aesop's fables are short and direct, and writers in each succeeding generation have embellished them to suit their era. In the same tradition, I have written this book, which follows the eBook version published in 2017, to address our current economic reality. In the new economy, achieving happiness (salvation) is elusive because materialism permeates all facets of life. This book,* The Crow and the Pitcher: A Retelling of Aesop's Fable, *is an allegory of the search for salvation, hampered by the distractions and negative influences of the modern era.*

Themes of salvation are prominent in ancient literature of the Mediterranean region. In the Egyptian epic of Heru and Set, Heru is the light of salvation that saves humankind from the darkness. In the New Kingdom, The Papyrus of Ani depicts the scribe at the moment of his judgment in his quest for everlasting life. Both Pythagoras and Plato dealt extensively with themes of virtue and salvation. Plato represents the self as a rational, immortal entity with free will. Plato warns us of the illusion of the material world that will lead us to the rocks.

Elements of the ancient world view are discernible in the plot, given the crow's struggles against the impending fate that he has ignored up to the last few moments. In the final hour, the crow's inherent materialistic tendencies hamper his efforts, and without divine intervention, there is no hope for him.

The emphasis on the alignment of Crow's head with the Sun at its crucial juncture with Earth is a reminder of the ancient mystical preoccupation with the June 21, summer solstice. The alignment is a warning of the approaching end of the growing season on the September 23 equinox—the last day of summer. In turn, the end of the Summer season anticipates a bountiful harvest.

Since salvation was foremost in the ancient world, consequently, so too was the preoccupation with the search for the elixir that would grant everlasting life. The elixir of life that the Crow seeks acquires a special significance as the process that preserves life and grants happiness. In virtue ethics of ancient societies, the balance between two extremes (the Golden Mean) is the quintessential remedy in the quest for eternal life. The old ethics taught that the addition of a deficiency restores balance and healing. The idea of rejuvenation and eternal life is symbolized by the elusive elixir, which is necessary to achieve balance and allows a process of physical renewal and spiritual awakening.

The Crow and the Pitcher *is a story about a race against time and a reminder of the fragility of life. As the winter season of life approaches, the bounty of the fall season is the best hope of surviving. However, like the crop before the harvest, it must be cultivated in the season of rejuvenation—the springtime of life.*

Crow's undying determination revealed through his search, is a character trait that helps him overcome his character flaw—the materialistic tendencies that hinder the crow. Nevertheless, even these ingrained negative attributes of Crow's life, play a role in his effort to defeat his most significant obstacle—his ego.

Chapter 1

When the crow awoke, he was soggy and still weary. It was already three hours past sunrise, and he was late. The hot summer sun bore down on his head with a vengeance. The air rising from the parched ground swirled around the bird's head like a suffocating shroud.

Crow could not remember ever being at the mercy of the elements unprepared. However, at the summer solstice, when the Sun had arrived at its longest day of the season and its highest intensity, he was imperiled. The bird's head was pointed due east and exposed to an infernal fury.

As he faced his most significant challenge, with not a drop of water to drink, Crow remained mired in folly. His thoughts were remote and unconcerned with his dire predicament. He dwelled on petty distractions—the material things of the Earth—that seemed more important than his well-being.

The precious elixir he desperately needed had never been a priority for Crow. He had never encountered this dilemma of an unfulfilled need, and because it was unlike the mundane situations with which he was familiar, he remained oblivious.

Always, the Crow had been diligent in his duties yet foolish in his aims, but nature had accommodated him. The many seasons of his pampered life lulled him into a sense of complacency, and Crow forgot his rational mind. He evolved to prefer living by chance alone while pursuing earthly pleasures.

At the summer solstice, when nature's seasonal clock chimed its warning of shorter days and diminishing fortunes ahead, it proved meaningless. Even as fate had surely spun its web day by day, Crow's thoughts gravitated to his wealth, glory, and honor. At the hour of his greatest challenge, not one of his precious material possessions gathered around him could fix his dilemma.

In the springtime of his life, Crow had come to appreciate the accrued years of good fortune as his destiny. The halcyon days were fulfilling beyond measure. Crow wallowed in the excesses of his material wealth—living by habit, understanding little, and even forgetting his life's purpose. On the best days, he made a nuisance of himself, cawing incessantly and intruding on the serene landscape. A selfish predisposition burdened the crow, and he was determined to possess all that he could.

Being black, and burdened with a forboding persona, the bird might seem deserving of his fate and not worthy of a passing thought. Indeed, he appeared to care nothing for the higher-order and even less for his self. However, the Crow's misgivings overshadowed his potential.

Crow had fearsome talons and a sharp beak, although he preferred the easy pickings from scavenging. He had a good physique with a wingspan from tip to tip surpassing three feet, but the crow cared nothing for the artistry of flight. He was content to carry himself by brute force, flapping hard and traveling straight. His feathers appeared disheveled and ill-suited to the bird. They were often in disarray and refracted the sunlight with a sullen gray cast. There was always a stark contrast between the bird and his surroundings, even in the shadows.

Despite all his potential, there was nothing more to the crow's persona than jet-black with an intermittent mottled grey sheen. Towards all these ends, Crow did aspire.

While his demeanor did impress a sense of foreboding on Crow, the forlorn character he radiated was unwarranted. Judging by the ethics of his time, he was no slacker. As a curious and a quick learner, the crow grew large and accumulated a bounty as well. In his collection, he had precious glassware, plastic ornaments, and an assortment of electronic gadgets. There was even a priceless jewel mounted on an exquisitely molded gold frame, inset with micro diamonds.

The crow, it seems, had navigated life's hazards with a brutal efficiency that was beyond ordinary. His internal clock had attuned to the stars. It awoke him before sunrise each morning to survey his terrain for the slimmest possibilities nature offered. He had persisted in this pattern until it became ingrained in his marrow. Never did the crow doubt that every new day would bring rewards like that of the previous day. Believing wholeheartedly in his abilities, the crow maintained the highest opinion of himself, and the fruits of his labors brought him the respect of his peers.

Chapter 2

On his fateful day—the hottest of the year—in the middle of a terrible drought, Crow's largesse and his bounty proved to be of no value. He stared death in the face, thirsty for the life-giving elixir.

Crow could barely lift the wings that hung in a tangled mass down to his talons. He posed the most pitiful sight. With his head bowed and his beak agape, he labored for each precious breath. In his weakened condition, Crow would not see the sunset. Finding the elixir his body craved would be the greatest accomplishment of his life.

Crow gathered his strength and began flapping laboriously. He anticipated taking flight as he had always done before. However, given his weakened state, it was inevitable that he would perish on the rocks below. Indeed, the bird did plunge headlong towards the ground.

Perhaps it was chance, but more aptly the work of an invisible hand that interceded. He landed in the scraggly brush, and miraculously, a sudden gust of wind did lift him into the air.

Crow could not perceive the lifeline nature had given him. His ignorance had dulled his cognitive senses and demoted his reason. As a creature of high culture and ingrained habit, he did not see a minor miracle in the making and given his demeanor; he would not have understood even if he had noticed.

Instinctively, the bird meandered his way towards his favorite place, a small creek nestled along a tree-lined ridge. Upon arriving there, Crow saw that the stream was bone dry.

In his weakened state, he fell onto the rocks in deep despair. Wisps of sand swirled around where the cold, refreshing pools of water once flowed. In the burning heat of the midmorning sun, the crow's efforts had made him more thirsty and much weaker.

His delusions shattered, and his will failed him. Crow paused in a state of delirium. His thoughts drifted to waiting out the waning hours of his life in the shade. He dreamed that mother Nature would intercede and bring him the elixir. Then he lay down as his eyes blurred.

Fate cared nothing for the crow's illusions, and time passed quickly—absent the crow. He lay still until reality reengaged Crow when the hot Sun seared his eye. The glowing, white orb was not a reminder of nature's severity but of Crow's foibles that had conjured this hard destiny. He recalled that he had enjoyed much better days under the same sun. Something had gone awry, but it was not the Sun.

Circumstances had worked against Crow, and his destiny converged towards a catastrophic state. His habitat was once fertile soil with a lush forest, but slowly, it had turned to dust. While Crow had benefited from years of abundance, he pursued fleeting material prosperity and remained immune to the terrible cost.

From within his shell, and fully indoctrinated, he saw and appreciated the wonders of Earth, but had never imagined he had a vital role to play. Crow was not born to dwell on haughty theories derived from conjecture. He had never thought of himself as belonging to nature. When the usual spring showers that nurtured the fields failed, Crow did not see the danger. The heavy smoke from blazing fires in the distance did not faze him. In truth, he did not notice that the fields that nourished him were now fallow.

Although it was late in coming, Crow's plight evoked regret. For the first time, he acknowledged the benefactor. His bountiful years without worry, when thoughts strayed to idle banter—away from reason and preparation to a focus on material pleasures—were all buffered by nature's benevolence. Still, there was a purpose in Crow's life. The ever-increasing collection of plastics below his perch testified to his diligent character. Although it was a testament to Crow's transgressions against nature, he believed it was a badge of courage.

In his few remaining hours, the Crow slowly grasped the truth, and he cried out with a weakened and confused spirit.

"This pain and sorrow do not suit me. Am I not that Crow, always noble in my bid for life, who has done his duty and collected his due reward? Yet, as my star shined bright before my eyes, my bid for life was merely an anchor in illusion that has led me to the rocks. But as sure as the Sun shines, I now know and see that my obligation must be to the greater good, for I am part of nature's tapestry."

Crow's half-hearted cry did not stop his appointment with fate. It approached steadily, marching to an unseen rhythm. With not a minute to spare, the crow vacillated between his illusions and reality. His carnal self evoked delusions of grandeur and conjured up Crow's denials of the higher-order, yet there occurred within his being a powerful surge of energy that overcame his indecision.

A short while before, it seemed so much better a proposition to lay in the shade and surrender, but Crow suddenly found himself airborne. There was no explanation for the bird's spontaneous flight from the rocks. His dire predicament had caused him to lose control of his ingrained pettiness, and now a superior reason controlled him.

In his flight, he soared on the warm currents of air and circled the sky like a bird of prey. He was majestic, but it was a sign of Crow's growing desperation. His flight was not the usual quirky motion that was more natural to him. Flapping vigorously, and expending prodigious amounts of energy was more his style.

In the heat of the moment, an unfamiliar instinct had surfaced. Crow could no longer waste time and energy on futile endeavors and pointless thoughts. A superior motive governed every move.

Crow was preoccupied with his singular purpose of finding the elixir and soared over the land with minimum effort. Suddenly, he noticed a tantalizing glint of light from the ground.

It was an antique pitcher sitting in the sun. Its circumference had an arcane, artfully crafted design. Crow had a working memory of his terrain, but the pitcher was unfamiliar to him. He recalled numerous occasions in the springtime as groups of strangers had gathered in celebration. He had watched their activities with interest then gorged on the morsels left behind. One of the strangers had forgotten the pitcher, and it had sat there for an extended period, exposed to the elements. The pitcher was once full of water, however, as the morning Sun rose, and shadows lengthened day after day, the water evaporated. The pitcher was now less than half full, and the water was difficult to reach.

Crow had spent more than four hours in the burning heat, looking for water. His will had brought him from the brink of disaster, but as he had finally found the life-giving substance, it was suddenly more elusive than ever. It seemed to Crow, that from the beginning of his ordeal when the specter of death had first surfaced, nature must have predetermined his end on this day.

Despite Crow's egotistical conclusion, the decision about his life was not his to consider. His spark of life that he thought belonged to him had unfolded according to a pattern established, long before he was born. As sure as there was a crow, there was

a corvid and circumstances that preceded, again and again, into infinity. Never could the crow have received the spark of life had he not been destined to be alive. Whether by fate or circumstance, the events occurring in his life mapped out in an unfolding series of events that made his life possible.

The crow cared nothing about philosophy—whether he should live or die was a secondary concern. While he lamented his approaching fate, all he understood was being alive, and all he knew was to live in the moment, doing what worked best for him. That decision was his most important choice. In reality, he had always lived life to the fullest extent he thought possible. In his most excellent hour, all the crow's faculties became engaged in fulfilling his destiny to be alive. His will succumbed to an unconscious guide and took on an important function the bird had never appreciated before.

Chapter 3

The crow stretched and strained in his attempts to taste the water. He felt energized. However, he soon realized that there was far too little of the water left in the pitcher. He could not reach a single drop of the precious elixir.

In rapid succession, he employed an array of skills that he believed would allow him to drink to his heart's content. He lurched forward, pulled back, and flapped his wings. He focused on quenching his thirst and getting on with the business of life. There were food to forage, sights to see, and oddities to investigate. However, again, and again, he failed to reach the life-giving water.

The crow was merely bumbling his way into a repetition of methods that differed insignificantly. Frustration had overcome his resolve and now governed his actions. His techniques were necessarily all similar approaches. A powerful push in one instance, followed a slightly more powerful thrust with a unique flap of his wings. That was all the bird could manage.

With each exertion, he anticipated the end of his desperate quest. For an extended period, the crow engaged in a brutal battle. With his talons extended, his wings flapping wildly and his feathers ruffled, Crow thrust himself at the pitcher, but it stood unmoved.

The crow failed miserably, but each time he reached deep within himself for an immeasurable strength and will that allowed him to persist.

The crow had no conscious idea of how to reach the water, nor did he have the luxury of time to sit and plan. He needed a solution now as his life depended on it. However, his thirst had taken control of his being, and he had thrown caution to the wind.

Despite the extended battle, the crow's only achievement was to have flapped his wings pointlessly and to have expended his precious energy. At last, Crow gave up from exhaustion. He began cawing loudly, exasperated by his failure.

He once again resigned himself to a fate for which he had not prepared. He lay down finally, and as his thoughts grew feeble, he set aside his worries. He began to lull away the remaining hours in the shade.

Crow's gaze drifted across the land, and he realized just how barren and parched it had become. The wind had blown much of the topsoil away, exposing the rocks and pebbles. It was a demoralizing sight to the humbled crow that had suddenly become attuned to his living environment.

He regretted the fact that he had failed himself and neglected his duty. From his humility, there emerged his waning courage, but it flowed from Divine Will so intense, that Crow immediately

became energized into resuming his solitary struggle—flapping and straining and cawing.

At the point of his greatest despair, a little thought came to him. It seemed like speculation, but doubtlessly it occurred because of the crow's newfound ability to discern the ultimate truth perceptible only to the rational mind. He had this ability within him, but always, the crow had preferred what his cognitive senses proposed. His knowledge was from his subconscious experience gathered during his many seasons of observing and learning from nature. It was his rational self acting on his behalf.

He picked up a pebble and dropped it into the pitcher, and observed with a keen interest moving his head from side to side. He then took another stone and released it into the pitcher. So it went—pebble after pebble went into the pitcher until at last, the crow observed the water level begin to rise.

Excited by the prospect, he quickened his pace and dropped a few more pebbles into the pitcher. At last, the water rose enough to reach the top, and Crow was able to quench his thirst and save his life.

* * *

MORAL

As our world is subject to powerful forces beyond our control, you will only rise to your highest aspiration. Live your life, always aiming for the highest ideal lest you fall to your lowest expectation.

. . . But above all, in the face of adversity, never give up.

GLOSSARY

Allegory: The expression by means of symbolic fictional figures and actions of truths or generalizations about human existence; also: an instance (as in a story or painting) of such expression. Work of written, oral, or visual expression that uses symbolic figures, objects, and actions to convey truths or generalizations about human conduct or experience. It encompasses such forms as the fable and parable.[1]

Antiquity: Ancient times; before the Middle Ages.[1]

Arcane: Known or knowable only to the initiate. Secret, mysterious, obscure. [1]

Ascend: To move upward; to rise from a lower level or degree.[1]

Aspiration: A strong desire to achieve something high or great.[1]

Circumference: The perimeter of a circle; the external boundary or surface of a figure or object.[1]

Cultivate: To improve by labor, care or study; refine the mind.

Delirium: A mental disturbance characterized by confusion, disordered speech, and hallucinations.

Demeanor: Behavior towards others; outward manner.

Divine will: Will of God, in contrast to human will.

Due diligence: An investigation of an opportunity. Research.

Elixir: The elixir of life or the elixir of immortality is often equated with the philosopher's stone. It is a mythical potion that grants the drinker eternal life and/or eternal youth, when drunk from a certain cup at a certain time of the year. The elixir of life was also believed to create life. It is related to the legend of Thoth (Egyptian name for the God of Wisdom) or Hermes Trismegistus (in Greek). He is believed to have achieved immortality after drinking "the white drops" (liquid gold). The elixir is mentioned in one of the Nag

Hammadi texts. Throughout the unfolding of history, alchemists in various ages and cultures searched for the formula of the elixir. [1]

Epic: Heroic; extending beyond the usual or ordinary, especially in size or scope. [1]

Equinox: An equinox occurs twice a year, around 20 March and 22 September. The word itself has several related definitions. The oldest meaning is the day when daytime and night are of approximately equal duration. [1]

Ethics: The systemizing of the process of living a good life. Moral philosophy. [1]

Exasperated: To become irritated or annoyed to the point of injudicious action. [1]

Exertion: To bring to bear with sustained effort or lasting effect. [1]

Fable: Narration intended to enforce a useful truth, especially one in which animals or inanimate objects speak and act like human beings. Unlike a folktale, it has a moral that is woven into the story and often explicitly formulated at the end. The Western fable tradition began with tales ascribed to Aesop. It flourished in the Middle Ages, reached a high point in 17th-century France in the works of Jean de La Fontaine, and found a new audience in the 19th century with the rise of children's literature. Fables also have ancient roots in the literary and religious traditions of India, China, and Japan. [1]

Foreboding: An omen, prediction, or presentiment especially of coming evil. [1]

Frivolous: Of little weight or importance. Lacking in seriousness. [1]

Mysticism: The term 'mysticism,' comes from the Greek word which means "to conceal." In the Hellenistic world, 'mystical' referred to "secret" religious rituals. In early Christianity the term came to refer to "hidden" allegorical interpretations of Scriptures and to hidden presences, such as that of Jesus at the

Eucharist. Only later did the term begin to denote "mystical theology," that included direct experience of the divine (See Bouyer, 1981). Typically, mystics, theistic or not, see their mystical experience as part of a larger undertaking aimed at human transformation (See, for example, Teresa of Avila, Life, Chapter 19) and not as the terminus of their efforts. Thus, in general, 'mysticism' would best be thought of as a constellation of distinctive practices, discourses, texts, institutions, traditions, and experiences aimed at human transformation, variously defined in different traditions.[3]

Persona: A person's perceived or evident personality, as that of a well-known official, actor, or celebrity; personal image; public role.[1]

Predicament: A difficult, perplexing, or trying situation.[1]

Refract: To break apart. The refraction of light through a prism results in the conversion of white light to rainbow colors.[1]

Rejuvenate: To make young or youthful again; give new vigor to.[1]

Salvation: The concept that claims it is God's will that human beings be saved from death. In religion, salvation is stated as the saving of the soul from sin and its consequences. It may also be called "deliverance" or "redemption" from sin and its effects. Salvation is considered to be caused either by the free will and grace of a deity. Religions often emphasize the necessity of both personal effort—for example, repentance and asceticism—and divine action (e.g. grace). Though there is some overlap in terminology, the divine act of saving a being (i.e., the soul) from biological death is properly called "resurrection", not "salvation", although the two distinct concepts are naturally related.

Within the field of theology dealing with salvation (*soteriology*), it has two related meanings. On the one hand it refers to the phenomenon of being saved by divine agency—such as the case in Christianity, Judaism and Islam. On the other it refers to the phenomenon of the soul being saved (as in "safe") from some unfortunate destiny. In the former, divine agency gives rise to the situation of the latter. However, devotion, petition, supplication and liturgical participation though considered integral to Roman Catholic and Eastern Orthodox Christianity are not considered enough alone to bring about salvation. Asceticism and repentance are advocated as essential from both a practical and sacramental point of view. Protestant Christianity (particularly evangelical Christianity) with its emphasis on sola fide asserts that salvation comes by way of grace through Jesus (Ephesians 2:8-9) and is effected by faith alone.—https://en.wikipedia.org/wiki/salvation

Specter: Something that haunts or perturbs the mind.[1]

Summer Solstice: In the northern hemisphere, the Summer solstice occurs around June 21. It marks the longest day of the year. The summer solstice occurs when the tilt of a planet's semi-axis, in either northern or southern hemispheres, is most inclined toward the star that it orbits. Earth's maximum axial tilt toward the Sun is 23° 26'. This happens twice each year, at which times the Sun reaches its highest position in the sky as seen from the north or the south pole.[3]

* * * * *

(1)   Merriam-Webster Dictionary

(2)   http://plato.stanford.edu/entries/mysticism/

(3)   Oxford Dictionaries

ABOUT THE AUTHOR

Zeph Ernest is the author and illustrator books for children, young adults and adults, including *Zari's Big Day, Volumes 1 and 2*; *The Crow and the Pitcher: A Retelling of Aesop's Fable* and *Adventures of Little David*.

Mr. Ernest is the founder of Z E Graphics, Inc., a graphic design, and self-publishing firm.

For over 20 years, Mr. Ernest has contributed to many college-level academic books as a Graphic Designer and illustrator.

He maintained a blog "The Declined Soul and the New Economy," for several years (2007–2014), which explored subjects of an ethical nature affecting the quality of life. He is an artist whose preferred medium is oil paints, and whose favorite subject matter is the landscape. Mr. Ernest also paints Geometric Abstract Art using acrylic paints.

Mr. Ernest graduated from Dartmouth College with a B.F.A. He later attended Boston University School of Graphic Design and Pace University School of Computer Science in New York.